For my son, Sebastian,
who chose these careers for himself.

Copyright © 1999 by NordSüd Verlag AG, CH-8005 Zürich, Switzerland.
First published in Switzerland under the title *Weißt du was ich werden will?*
English translation copyright © 1999 by NorthSouth Books Inc., New York 10016.

First published in the United States, Great Britain, Canada, Australia, and
New Zealand in 1999 by North-South Books Inc., New York 10016, an imprint of
NordSüd Verlag AG, CH-8005 Zürich, Switzerland. First paperback edition published 2001.

Distributed in the United States by NorthSouth Books Inc., New York 10016.

Library of Congress Cataloging-in-Publication Data
Horn, Peter.
[Weisst du was ich werden will? English]
When I grow up... / by Peter Horn; illustrated by Cristina Kadmon;
translated by Rosemary Lanning.
p. cm.

Summary: Sebastian the turtle tells his father about all the jobs
he might do when he grows up, from fireman to skydriver, and agrees
that being a father might be the best of all.

[1. Occupations–Fiction. 2. Fathers and sons–Fiction.
3. Turtles–Fiction] I. Kadmon, Cristina, ill.
II. Lanning, Rosemary. III. Title.
PZ7.H78225Wh 1999
[E]–dc21 99-18976

A CIP catalogue record for this book
is available from The British Library.

Printed in China by Toppan Leefung Printing Limited., Dongguan, April 2013.

ISBN: 978-0-7358-1418-9 (paperback) 10 9 8 7 6

www.northsouth.com

When I Grow Up...

by Peter Horn

illustrated by Cristina Kadmon

translated by

Rosemary Lanning

North South

A beautiful summer day was drawing to its end.
Sebastian had played with his friends all day long.
They had run races with Theo the snail . . .

spun on their shells until they were dizzy,
and splashed around in a cool green pond.

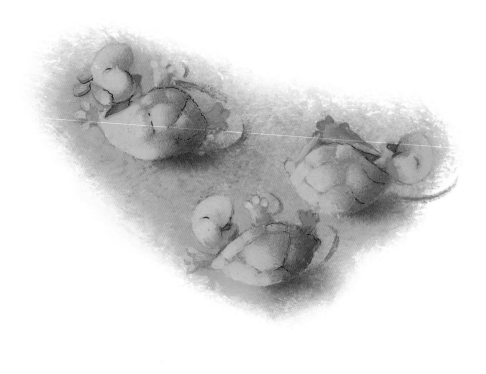

When they were hungry, they crawled into a strawberry patch and munched the sweet red fruit until their faces were thoroughly smeared with juice.

Then it was time to go home, so they said good-bye and went their separate ways.

Sebastian snuggled down beside his father on soft grass that was still warm from the afternoon sun. Stars twinkled in the sky above them, but Sebastian didn't feel tired enough to go to sleep just yet.

"Do you know what I want to be when I grow up?" he said.

His father looked surprised. "Have you decided already?"

"Yes," said Sebastian. "I want to be a fireman. I would wear a bright red uniform and a shiny silver helmet. And if you had a fire, I would come and put it out for you."

"It's good to know you'd save us," said his father.

"That's not the only job I could do!" said Sebastian.
He was getting excited now, and his words came
tumbling out. "I could be a pirate!"

"Oh dear," said his father. "Pirates are horrible. Ter-
rors of the sea!"

"Don't worry," said Sebastian, nuzzling his father's
nose. "I would be a nice pirate, not a horrible one.
I wouldn't sink any ships."

"What would you do?"

"I'd sail away to desert islands," said Sebastian. "And if I found any treasure, I would give it away, to the poor."

"That would be kind of you."

"Or I could be a deep-sea diver. How about that? I would dive right down to the bottom of the sea and have races with the fish. They must run faster than Theo the snail!"

"I'm sure they do," said Father.

Father and son gazed up at the moon, which glowed softly like a paper lantern in the sky. Sebastian felt as if the sandman was sending him to sleep, but he tried not to yawn. Another idea had just occurred to him, and it was so good that he had to tell his father.

"I could be a sky diver," Sebastian said. "I'd ask a bird to carry me up into the sky, and I'd jump off his back and float down with a parachute. Then I could tell you what the world looks like from up there."

"I'd like that," said his father, "and I'd think you were very brave."

Now Sebastian was very, very tired. He struggled to keep his eyes open as he asked his father: "What did you want to be when you were little?"

"Mmm, let me think," said Father. He looked fondly at Sebastian. "I always wanted to be a father," he said. "I hoped to have a son who would make me proud, whatever he did. As proud as I am of you."

Father Turtle gently stroked his son's back.

Sebastian gave a happy sigh and tucked his head snugly inside his shell, ready for sleep.

"And I'd like to grow up to be just like you," he murmured drowsily.

As the warm night wind carried Sebastian's words away across the meadow, he was already fast asleep.